To My Grandchildren

May you enjoy, love and
respect the water as I do.
Stay safe, little seals!

Love, Mimi / Grandma

WATER SAFETY

PUT A RING OF SAFETY AROUND YOUR CHILD

SUPERVISION • SWIMMING LESSONS
WATER SAFETY • BARRIERS • CPR

- SUPERVISION: Do not leave your child alone in, on or around the water as a tragedy can happen in seconds. Never assume someone is watching your child, designate an adult as a "pool watcher" at social events and do not rely on floatation devices to protect your child.

- SWIMMING LESSONS: Swimming lessons will keep your child safer, but be sure to up-grade your child's swimming skills every year.

- WATER SAFETY: Education is important, not only for you but for your child. Make sure you and your child know and follow the safety rules. You must lead by example.

- BARRIERS: Pool fences, locked gates, windows and doors are all part of your child's safety ring.

- CPR: Take infant/child/adult CPR courses and up-date every year. Accidents do not make appointments; every family needs to be prepared.

Swim Safe
Little Seals

A Child's Introduction to Water Safety

Therese Cullen Seal and Jill MacGregor
Illustrations by Bob Donovan

www.sealswimschool.com

ISBN-13 Digit 978-0-9774062-0-3
ISBN-10 Digit 0-9774062-0-2

Library of Congress Number: 2006920780

First Edition — 2006
Second Edition — 2007

These little seals just love to play
They dive off rocks and splash all day.

"Safety First" they always say
Let's learn the rules Safe Seals obey.

NEVER SWIM ALONE!

8   Never, never swim alone, even if you're big and grown.

Don't go swimming on your own
A Safe Seal never swims alone.

Always look before you swim
Never run and jump right in.

There might be a rock or limb
Safe Seals look before they swim.

I jumped in headfirst where it's not too deep.
Next time I'll look before I leap.

SAFE SEALS ALWAYS OBEY EACH RULE.

MY REPORT CARD

GRADES

Never Swim Alone	A
Look Before You Swim	A
Wear a Safety Vest in the Boat	A
Dive Right (Look Below)	A
Help, But Don't Jump In	A
Obey all Safety Rules	

SEAL
SWIM SCHOOL

SEAL
OF
APPROVAL

Whenever seals go to the pool
They should follow every rule
'Cause getting hurt is never cool.

A VEST IS BEST!

**When skiing or boating it's always best
To wear a Safety Water Vest.**

Put one on before you go
'Cause Safe Seals 'wear a vest' you know.   15

**Make sure it's deep
and safe to swim**

**Safe seals never
dive right in.**

**Before you dive look down below
Someone could be there, you know.**

16

HELP, DON'T JUMP

When seals need help
Don't swim to them,

A rope or paddle to extend
Safe Seals help but don't jump in.

If something happens in the pool
There are some things you can do.

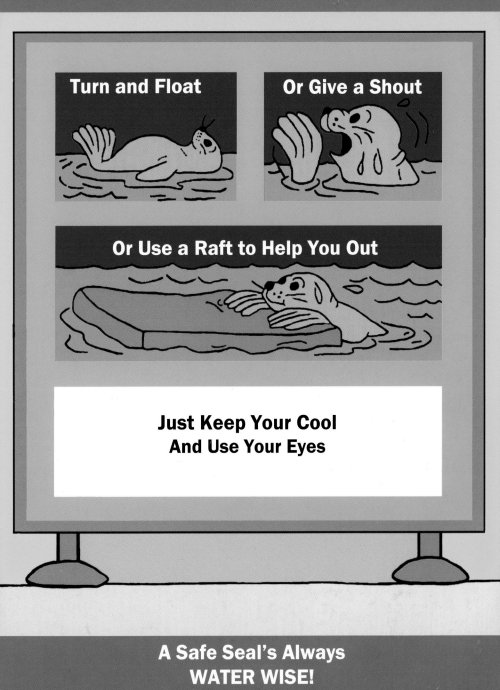

SAFE SEAL TIP REVIEW

Always look before you swim
Never run and jump right in.

SAFE SEAL TIP REVIEW

**Don't go swimming on your own
A Safe Seal never swims alone.**

SAFE SEAL TIP REVIEW

A VEST IS BEST!

**When skiing or boating it's always best
To wear a Safety Water Vest.**

**Turn and float or give a shout
Or use a raft to help you out.**

**Just keep your cool and use your eyes
A Safe Seal's always water wise!**

SAFE SEAL TIP REVIEW

NEVER SWIM ALONE!
Never, Never swim alone even if you're big and grown.

When seals need help, don't swim to them.
A rope or paddle to extend,
Safe Seals help but don't jump in.

**Mommy, Daddy, latch the door
The pool's a place that I adore.**

Keep me safe when I jump in
Stay close by each time I swim.

At last, Little Seal, your lesson's through
Now, you know what Safe Seals do.

BE LIKE THEM AND KEEP THEIR RULES

IN BOATS

AT LAKES

OR IN THE POOLS

MY DIPLOMA!
You can be a Safe Seal like me!

**SAFE SEALS ALWAYS
OBEY EACH RULE.**

THERESE CULLEN SEAL holds a B.S. in Education from the University of South Florida. She is a member of the United States Swim School Association, an American Red Cross Water Safety Instructor Trainer and has been a certified lifeguard for over 30 years. Therese has taught swimming and water safety to thousands of children in the Tampa Bay area. She developed a love for swim instruction while growing up in Tarpon Springs, Florida. Therese gave her first swim lesson at the age of nine at Wall Springs and was a competitive swimmer for most of her youth.

Therese founded Seal Swim School in 1979 and her business has developed into one of the largest learn to swim programs in Florida. She has attended and spoken at National and International conferences all over the world. Her dedication to children, water safety and swim instruction has established her as a leader in the swim school industry.

Therese resides at her lakefront home in Odessa, Florida. She enjoys spending time with her five children, their spouses and her grandchildren.

JILL MACGREGOR and her family live in Tarpon Springs, Florida. Jill introduced her "little pups" to the world of water at Seal Swim School. Water safety gets her stamp of approval and is the source of inspiration for the pages found in this book. As a former lifeguard, Jill takes water safety very seriously, but believes kids can have fun learning the rules. As a writer, more of Jill's poetry can be found in gift books published by Andrews McMeel Publishing, HarperSanFrancisco of Harper Collins, Harmony Books of New York, and Ideals Publications-Guideposts.

BOB DONOVAN (1921–2002), a self-taught artist, began his career as a cartoonist after serving in the Marines during World War II. While working for Leatherneck magazine in Washington D.C., Bob met Fred Lasswell, creator of the "Barney Google and Snuffy Smith" comic strip. Bob became Lasswell's assistant and worked on "Barney Google and Snuffy Smith" for over 30 years. During this time, Bob also created his own strip "Biddie and Bert", about a retired couple, which ran for about 3 ½ years.

After retiring from the "Barney Google" strip, Bob started drawing educational comic books from his home studio in Tampa, Florida. He has drawn comic books for elementary school children such as "Meet the Bank", "McGruff's Surprise Party", and "Share the Water".

Reprints of Bob's cartoons have appeared in numerous publications including the New York Times, the Buffalo Evening News, Look magazine, and Life magazine.